W9-CKG-500

SCOTT, FORESMAN FIRST TALKING STORYBOOK BOX

A is for Alphabet by Cathy, Marly, and Wendy

Anatole by Eve Titus

Angelo the Naughty One by Helen Garrett

Benjie by Joan M. Lexau

Chicken Licken

Frances Face-Maker by William Cole

Harry the Dirty Dog by Gene Zion

Humbug Witch by Lorna Balian

Jack and the Beanstalk

Little Bear's Pancake Party by Janice

Mickey's Magnet by Franklyn M. Branley and Eleanor K. Vaughan

Mother Goose Rhymes

Over in the Meadow by John Langstaff

Straight Up by Henry B. Lent

The House That Jack Built

The Little Rabbit Who Wanted Red Wings by Carolyn Sherwin Bailey

The Shoemaker and the Elves

The Tale of the Flopsy Bunnies by Beatrix Potter

Timothy Turtle by Al Graham

What Mary Jo Shared by Janis Udry

Where's Andy? by Jane Thayer

WHERE'S ANDY

Story by
JANE THAYER

Pictures by
Meg Wohlberg

WILLIAM MORROW AND COMPANY
New York   1954

Special Scott, Foresman and Company Edition
for *Scott, Foresman First Talking Storybook Box*

Copyright **1954** by William Morrow and Company, Inc.
All rights reserved.
Printed in the United States of America.

Library of Congress Catalog Card Number: **54-6259**

This special edition is printed and distributed by Scott, Foresman and Company
by special arrangement with William Morrow and Company, Inc.,
425 Park Avenue South, New York, New York, 10016.

One day Andy was playing
in the yard when he heard
Mother call from the back
door. "Andy!" Mother called
again. She wanted to find out
where he was.

3

Andy started to answer, but
then he happened to think
what fun it would be if Mother
had to come and find him. So

4

instead of answering, he slipped
behind a big apple tree.

When Andy didn't answer,
Mother came out to find him.

She said, "Where is that boy?"

She looked
all around.
She looked
behind the
lilac bush.

She looked
in the water-
ing can.

Then she looked at the big
apple tree and she thought she
saw something like a piece of
Andy's ear sticking out.

"Could he be behind that tree, I wonder?" Mother said thoughtfully.

As Mother went around the tree trunk Andy went around faster, and very quietly he got behind Mother.

Mother said, "I guess Andy must have gone into the house. I'll look in the house." She went back into the house and Andy went along very quietly, right behind her.

"I don't see him anywhere in
the kitchen," said Mother. "I'll
see if he is in the bedroom."

She went into the bedroom.
Andy went into the bedroom
very quietly, right behind her.

"He isn't here. Could he be
in the closet?" said Mother.
She opened the closet door and

looked behind all the clothes.
"No, he isn't in the closet,"
she said.

"I know. He's under the bed. You come out from under that bed!" said Mother, shaking her finger. No Andy came out from under the bed. Mother got down on her hands and

knees and peered under the bed. "I see some dust," she said, "and I see a bedroom slipper. but I certainly do not see Andy."

"I bet he's under this quilt!"
Mother cried.

She felt the quilt all
over. "I can't find any
bump that feels like Andy!"

"Where can that boy be?" Mother said. "He must be hiding behind my beautiful flowered chintz drapes. You come out from behind those drapes at once!"

She shook out the folds of the flowered chintz drapes. She looked behind every one. But she didn't find Andy draped in the flowered chintz drapes.

"Did he crawl under the rug?" Mother said. She stooped and turned up the edge of the rug and looked way under.

Andy scrunched down behind her. She looked so funny looking under the rug, he couldn't help giggling.

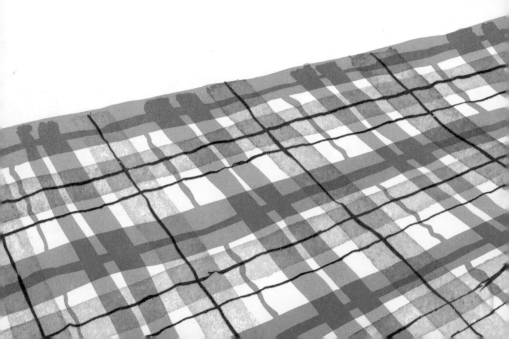

"Did I hear someone giggle just then?" said Mother, very surprised. "Who can be giggling around this place—there's nobody here but me. I guess I didn't hear a giggle. Now where else could Andy be?"

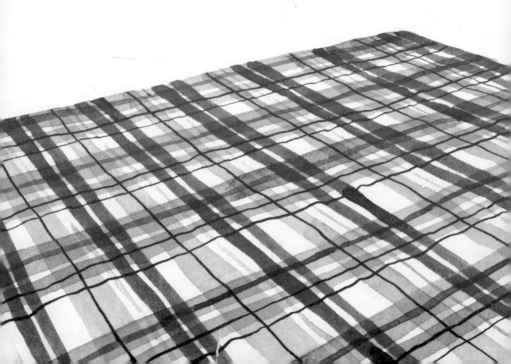

Mother went into the living room. "Perhaps he was sitting in this chair and slipped down behind the cushion. I'd better look!" Mother said. She pulled the cushion out of the chair.

She found her thimble
down in the chair.

   She found three pennies,

four marbles,

   a pair of scissors,

the key to the back door,

   and an airplane.

But not a sign of Andy.

"I wonder if I threw him away by mistake!" exclaimed Mother, quite worried. "I'll look in the wastepaper basket." She reached down into the basket and rummaged around, but there was no Andy in the wastebasket.

"Oh, I know," Mother said. "He must be in this desk drawer." She pulled out the drawer. She pulled out all the drawers and looked in every one.

No Andy!

"Then he's hiding inside a book," Mother said. "I'll shake the pages of this book and maybe he'll fall out." She turned the book upside down. Andy didn't fall out.

Andy couldn't help giggling again, because she thought he was hiding in a book.

"I heard someone giggling again!" cried Mother loudly, listening. "Now who in the world could that be, giggling? And *where* has that Andy gone to?"

Her eye fell on her sewing basket. "Hmm," Mother said. "I wonder. Could he be hiding in my sewing basket? That boy will sit on a pin if he doesn't watch out." She tiptoed over to the sewing basket. She threw up the lid. But Andy was not inside.

"I'll go back to the kitchen," said Mother with a sigh. She went back to the kitchen.

"Isn't it funny?" said Mother. "It sounds as if someone were walking around this house *be-hind* me. Who *could* it be? And where on earth is Andy?"

"Maybe he's on a cupboard shelf," she said. She opened the cupboard door. "Yoo-hoo!" called Mother. Andy was not in the mixing bowl or down in the flour bin.

"Oh, I hope he didn't go down the drain in the sink!" Mother said anxiously. "Are you down in that pipe, Andy? You come right up!" Andy didn't come up.

"I have looked everywhere," said Mother in despair. "He isn't in the closet. He isn't under the bed. He isn't draped in my beautiful flowered chintz drapes."

"He didn't crawl under the rug or slip down behind a cushion. I certainly didn't throw him away and he's nowhere in my desk drawer. He isn't hiding in a book and he's not in my sewing basket. He doesn't seem to be in the bowls or bins.

He didn't go down the drain. I guess he has gone away," Mother said. "I'll tell that Andy a few things when he comes home! Now I'll just sit down in this chair and wait till he comes."

Andy quickly sat down in the chair first, and Mother started to sit right down on top of him.

"Murder!" screeched Mother, jumping up. "What am I sit-ting on?"

"Me!" said Andy, in the chair.

"Where in the world have you been?" exclaimed Mother, whirling around.

"Right behind you wherever you went. And that was me giggling, too," said Andy, giggling some more.

"Well, the very idea," said Mother, "of fooling me like that! You come here and be spanked."

"No!" shouted Andy, giggling louder than ever.

"Then I guess I'll have to hug you," said Mother. "I'm so glad to see you again!"

And that is just what she did.